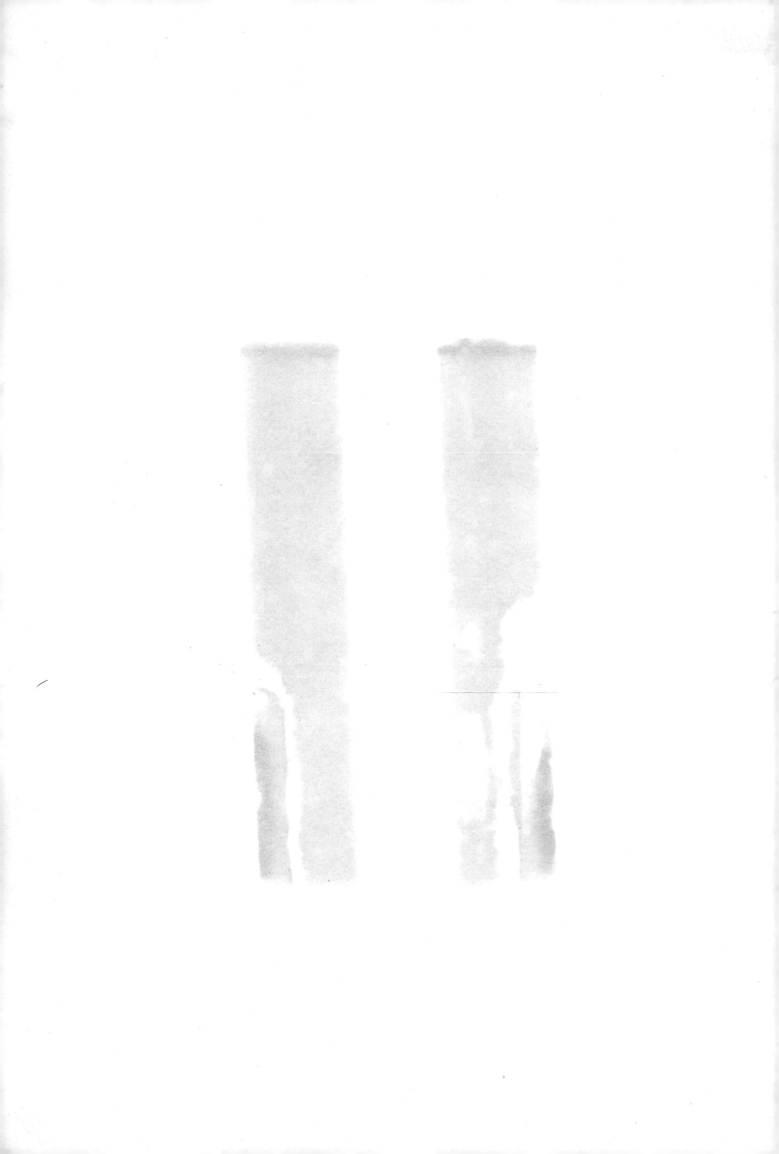

sun & moon

A GIANT LOVE STORY

LISA DESIMINI

THE BLUE SKY PRESS

An Imprint of Scholastic Inc.

FOR ALL GREAT COUPLES

The Blue Sky Press is a registered trademark of Scholastic Inc.

Library of Congress catalog card number: 98-28836   ISBN 0-590-18720-8

11 10 9 8 7 6 5 4 3 2 1   9/9 0/0 01 02 03 04

Printed in the United States of America   36

First printing, February 1999   Designed by Kathleen Westray

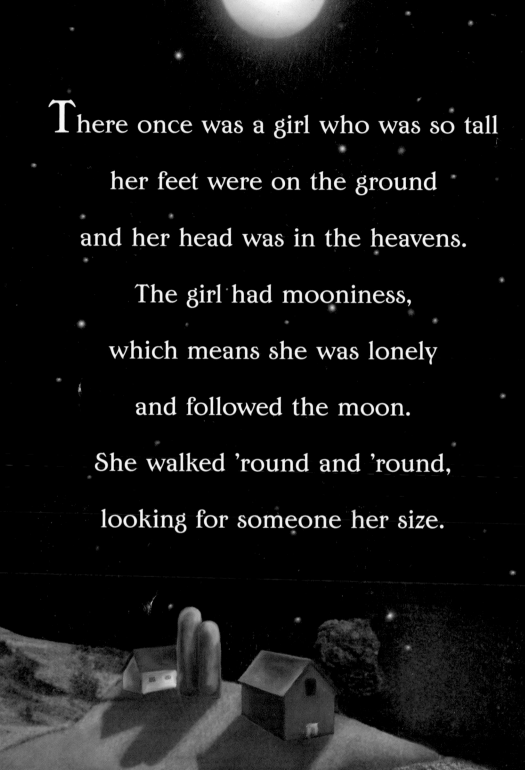

There once was a girl who was so tall

her feet were on the ground

and her head was in the heavens.

The girl had mooniness,

which means she was lonely

and followed the moon.

She walked 'round and 'round,

looking for someone her size.

There once was a boy who was so tall

his feet were on the ground

and his head was in the clouds.

The boy was afraid of the dark,

so he followed the sun.

He was always looking,

but for as far as he could see,

there was no one else his size.

The boy and girl

were as far apart

as the sun and moon —

as far apart as

two people could be.

They were giants
on the same planet,
but they had never met.

The girl bathed alone in the ocean.

Animals watched over her as she slept.

The boy bathed with water squeezed from clouds.

Birds kept him warm as he slept.

The girl collected shooting stars and kept them in her pockets,
wishing she could show them to someone.

The boy made shadow puppets on the ground,
wishing he could share them with a friend.

Because they were giants, the boy and girl could see trouble from far away. The boy rescued boats from rough water.

The girl shook stars out of her pockets to help lost travelers
find their way. There was always something to do.

But the girl was sad.

And so was the boy.

"I wish I had

someone to love,"

they both said

at the same moment.

And the sun and moon

heard them.

The moon shined

its light even brighter

to guide the girl,

and the sun spread

its warmth

to lead the boy.

The sun and moon, so far apart, were moving closer.

The girl began
to dream
of sunshine.

The boy began
to dream
of moonbeams.

Until suddenly, one day,
the sun and moon came together —
an eclipse.

The boy and girl were face to face!

The girl held up a star, for the boy
who was afraid of the dark.

The boy covered the sun with a cloud, for the girl
who was not used to the bright light.

The boy and girl learned

to laugh,

and they learned

to play.

They stopped walking in circles.

Instead they talked

while the sun and moon

moved across the sky.

They were giants on the same planet . . .

. . . and they belonged together.